THE REAL THIEF

THE REAL THIEF

STORY AND PICTURES BY
WILLIAM STEIG

Farrar, Straus and Giroux ◊ New York

To Maggie, Melinda, and Francesca

Gawain stood on guard outside the new Royal Treasury, his dangerous halberd gleaming in the bright sun. The pavement was a bit hot for his feet and he raised first one, ever so slightly, and then the other. Some tourists came by. Gawain held his head proudly on his long neck and his chest expanded in his red and gold uniform as they photographed him.

When the tourists had moved on, Gawain found himself wishing for his old way of life—swimming in his pond, tilling his bed of herbs, raising prize cabbages and string beans, and drafting plans for strikingly original buildings. He had always dreamed of becoming a great architect and he had visions of a new palace he was sure the King would love. It would be oviform—that is, it would have the ideal shape of the egg.

Being Chief Guard of the newly built Royal Treasury made him an important goose, but the job bored him. Then why had he accepted it? He had been chosen for the post by King Basil the bear because of his upright, trustworthy character, and he had accepted because he couldn't possibly have refused. He loved the rough, gruff, fatherly King. His heart warmed in the King's presence. He admired his strength. He loved the smell of honey on him, on his fur, on his robes, on his breath. He wanted to please him, to stay forever in his gruff, good graces. Everyone did. Basil was a popular king.

For the sake of uniformity, three other geese—Harvey, Garvey, and Wetmore—had been chosen to take turns with Gawain standing guard in front of the treasury, but only Gawain and the King had keys. The geese had worked

out and carefully rehearsed a brief and unpretentious cere-
mony for the changing of the guard. At the appointed time
the two guards would honk twice and the one being relieved
would waddle out as his alternate sidled in.

Once a day Gawain had to unlock the massive door,
shove it open with his shoulder, and go into the treasure
house to make sure that all was in apple-pie order. Then he
would lock up again.

The King himself now and then went to the treasure
house, and he opened the massive door with a mere touch.
He put things in, or he took things out—jewels, medallions,

precious crowns of historical interest, money garnered as taxes for running the government. Whenever he was too harried with irksome affairs of state, or on nights when he couldn't stop the stream of his thoughts and fall asleep, he would go there and count gold pieces and whatever else he felt needed counting. It soothed his nerves and he always slept well afterward.

Naturally, whenever the King removed anything from the treasury, or added anything to it, he informed Gawain of the changes. Gawain always enjoyed these short conferences with the King; he looked forward to them.

For a long time, nothing was amiss. All was peaceful, though boring. But one day, in his routine checkup, it seemed to Gawain that the pile of rubies was smaller than it should have been. He counted hastily and went flapping and running to the King to report that something was missing. King Basil calmed him. He put down his pot of honey, wiped his fingers, and together they went back to the treasury.

By the light of a lamp they carefully counted the rubies, both calling out the numbers. Sure enough, there were only 8,643 of the red gems when there should have been 8,672. Twenty-nine rubies had disappeared!

King Basil and his Chief Guard of the Royal Treasury

looked at each other. The King lifted the lamp and held it to Gawain's face. "How could anyone have gotten in here?" he asked. "Only you and I have keys. Could you possibly have left the door open by mistake?"

"Oh, no, your highness," said Gawain, "I'm always careful. I check, I double-check, and I re-double-check. Sometimes my mind may wander, but my eyes are always wide open. I see left and I see right at the same time. I don't see so well forward, but no one can get by me without passing either my left eye or my right one."

Harvey, Garvey, and Wetmore were summoned and each came running, holding his halberd, and stood at atten-

tion in front of the King. They were questioned in turn. No, they said, if anything out of the ordinary had happened, they would surely have reported it, for that was their duty. Those who usually passed by had passed. There had been an occasional foreign sightseer. Nothing else. No one had come near the door.

The locks were examined by expert locksmiths. They were sound. Gawain assured the King that he would be doubly careful after this. And doubly careful he was, even triply. He kept constantly alert, avoided daydreams, bearing in mind his great responsibility to his king and the kingdom, and he scrutinized every creature that passed, even if it was only a haphazard, meandering butterfly. He cautioned Harvey, Garvey, and Wetmore to do the same. Whenever the guard was changed and he waddled out as another sidled in, he warned: "Be watchful!"

And they were watchful. But in the next several days, first a great many gold pieces were missing, and after that some precious silver ornaments, and *then* the prize of the treasury, the world-famous Kalikak diamond!

King Basil was frantic. He strode up and down, his purple robe dragging behind him. He had Gawain and his helpers on the carpet in front of his throne and he questioned them closely over and over. Their answers were always the same. They had been on constant duty. At night the guard had been doubled to make certain there was no nodding or dozing. And certainly no sleeping—their heads were never under their wings. Gawain, the Chief, had made his round not once daily but twice, checking the treasures with scrupulous care. There was no way to account for the disappearances.

Once during the questioning, his webbed feet deep in the pile of the King's red carpet, Gawain had the impression that the King looked at him a bit too searchingly, a bit suspiciously in fact. He quivered, and returned a clear, un-blinking gaze with his button-like eyes. He loved this large, warm, furry king with the fat furry ears who wore his royal purple so casually. He understood his being upset, but he was offended.

"Begging your honorable indulgence," he said with a tinge of irony in his tone, "isn't it in the realm of possibility that your regal self made a royal mistake? I humbly kiss your warm and furry feet and I hope you don't think me dis-respectful if I suggest that mayhap you yourself removed some of those treasured objects and, preoccupied as you are with the lofty responsibilities of a monarch, have forgotten you did so."

This tactless statement seemed to Basil wholly uncalled for. He stared at the insolent goose and the brown fur bris-tled on his nape. "I know what I'm doing, Gawain," he roared. "The King makes no mistakes!"

"Excuse me," said Gawain, changing his tone. "How dared I!" And he snapped his bill shut and hung his head.

The unaccountable turn of events had King Basil flabber-gasted. He hated this problem that had no solution. He called a special meeting of his Royal Cabinet and asked for their opinion.

"Who has keys?" asked his Prime Minister, Adrian the cat, though he already knew the answer.

"Only my royal self and Gawain," answered Basil.

"The treasury is built of solid stones, well fitted and a foot thick," said the Prime Minister, "and it has inner walls of good heavy oak. The floor is also of stone, and the building has no windows, no chimney, and no cellarway. The thick wooden door is banded with riveted iron and locked with four sturdy locks. None of the locks is broken or shows signs of having been tampered with. They've been examined by the best locksmiths. Since your highness would never rob his extraordinary self, who else could it have been but Gawain? No one here believes in ghosts."

"It was not Gawain," said the King firmly. "He is an honorable goose, as everyone knows. I trust him as much as I do myself. The fact is, I love him as I would a son."

"Love him like a son, if you will," said Adrian with visible envy, "but as Prime Minister I cannot be guided by such irrational sentiments. Treasure is missing from the treasury —of that there is no question. There is no access or egress except through the door; no locks have been broken, and only you and your beloved goose have keys. These are facts. The culprit has to be either Gawain or, begging your lofty forgiveness, yourself. Since you have no reason to despoil your own treasury, and since it is unthinkable for you to be wrong about any earthly thing, Gawain is the only logical answer to the question of who did it." Adrian made an obsequious bow, and his tail rose, wavered, and arched over as he added in official Latin, *"Quod erat demonstrandum."*

The King didn't know what to say in response to the Prime Minister's flawless reasoning. He trusted the operations of Adrian's mind more than he did his own instinct. He sent his councilors away and slumped in his throne, dejected. Having listened to an opinion he didn't really believe but was forced to respect, he grew confused and fell into muddled ponderings. His mind was crossed with wayward shadows and he brooded, and the more he brooded the more he became darkly convinced that his beloved Gawain, no matter his bright, innocent eyes, and despite his untarnished record, was a thief, and trusting him had been a doltish error.

Gawain, at home, in a sleep troubled by worries, was rousted out of bed at midnight, allowed one minute to get dressed, and dragged to the castle dungeon. There he was stripped of his red and gold uniform and given the drab garb of a prisoner. His halberd and his keys were taken away and

he was flung into a damp cell by rude wardens. He sat in the cell on the cold stone floor in a state of shock, wondering why a good goose who had done his duty was now confined in a dirty dungeon.

In the gray, sunless morning a search of his house and his land was made. Experts went through his papers—his diaries, his letters, his blueprints—studying them for clues. The bottom of his pond was gone over by divers. Nothing that shouldn't have been there was found anywhere on Gawain's property.

"He's hidden the loot somewhere," said the Prime Minister. "I know he has. I recommend that we bring him to trial and find out where."

King Basil agreed.

A trial was held a few days later. Gawain was brought to the courthouse between two wardens. The familiar town looked the same as always, with its friendly houses and its wide, tidy streets; but to Gawain, being hauled through these gracious streets by officers of the law, it was strange that it should look the same.

In court Gawain declined the help of a lawyer. He felt he needed none since he was innocent. The trial was ridiculous, as everyone would soon see. He sat waiting for the nonsense to begin.

The whole town crowded into the courthouse. They all knew Gawain. They were his friends, his admirers. Some had known him his whole lifetime and understood his character well. He had gone to school with some of them. They had romped together, shared, enjoyed things. They were all dear to him and he was a favorite with them. The town was aghast at the charges that had been laid against their beloved goose and had been muttering about it for the past few days, ever since the trial had been announced. Gawain a thief? How utterly out of the question! However he had come to be accused of this dastardly crime, the luster of his name would surely be preserved.

King Basil sat in the judge's seat, a tired look on his
face. Over his head hung the big brass scales, brightly pol-
ished, that symbolized justice. Gawain stood alone in a
cleared space before him. Many of the spectators had no
seats.

After Ezra, the bailiff, called the court to order, King
Basil got right down to the business at hand. He looked at
Gawain and asked, "Do you swear to tell only the truth?"

"I do," said Gawain indignantly.

"Are you the Chief Guard of the Royal Treasury?"

"You know I am," said Gawain, "you appointed me yourself."

"Is it a fact," shouted the King, "that twenty-nine rubies, one hundred three gold ducats, several silver ornaments, and the Kalikak diamond are missing from the treasury?"

"It is," said Gawain. "No need to shout." He had spent a sleepless and agitated night and he was exhausted, but he managed to hold his head high. He glanced at his friends and they looked back reassuringly. He saw the beaver John, Martin the goat, Louisa May the bulldog, who had named her first son after him, his fellow geese—Harvey, Garvey, Wetmore, Jarvis, and Jeb—and many others; and their kind looks gave him courage.

"Are you aware," said the King, "that the Kalikak diamond alone is worth millions, and that because of this thieving we will not be able to build the opera house we had planned, and that, furthermore, taxes will have to be raised?"

"No, I wasn't aware of that," said Gawain. "I've had other things to think about." Everyone was attentive. They hadn't considered the consequences of the thefts.

"Who else guards the Royal Treasury?" asked the King.

"My good friends Harvey, Garvey, and Wetmore."

"Do they have keys to the treasury?" Basil asked.

"No," said Gawain.

"Could anyone get into the treasury without keys?"

"No," said Gawain. "The door is the only way in or out and it is always locked."

"Who besides myself had keys to the treasury?" asked Basil.

"I did," said Gawain.

"Did anyone else have keys?"

"No," said Gawain. There were astonished murmurs among the spectators and King Basil had to rap for order. "Tell the court this," he said. "Did you ever give your keys to anyone else? Were they ever out of your possession?"

"Never," said Gawain. "They were always hanging at my belt by day, and at night they were under my pillow."

"Do you think it possible that in some mysterious way the treasure left the treasure house by itself?" A few involuntary titters were heard at the King's question.

"No!" said Gawain heatedly.

"Did you ever forget to lock the door?"

"Absolutely no," answered Gawain.

"You agree with me then," the King went on, "that only you and I had access to the royal treasures since only we had keys. Do you think it likely that *I* stole those things, thereby robbing myself and my own subjects?"

Tense silence in the crowd.

"I no longer know what to think," said Gawain. "I only know that I stand here falsely accused. I cannot vouch for your highness, only for myself. It wasn't I!"

Gawain could hear the spectators gasp. He understood that his audacity had shocked them. King Basil himself was furious. "Much of our wealth is missing," he roared, "and there are only two who could have taken it, you or your king. You stand there boldly denying you did it, and to cover up your own guilt you are willing to imply that your king might be the thief!"

Gawain could smell the honey on the King's breath. "I am innocent," he said.

The King pointed at Gawain and addressed the crowd. "You see before you a goose who has deceived us all. We trusted him and he violated our trust. No one could possibly be the thief but he." He looked at Gawain with contempt and said, "I hereby accuse you of stealing royal treasure, and I further lay a charge of perjury upon you! You swore to tell the truth."

"I am an honest goose," said Gawain, and he turned to his friends for confirmation. They failed to meet his eye. They looked embarrassed. He was horrified at what he read on their faces. It was clear they had stopped believing in him. The evidence brought out by the King had convinced them that he was guilty!

"You are a disgrace to this kingdom!" said Basil, snarling with disgust. That simple statement, so cruelly delivered, froze in Gawain's head. He grew confused. Were these things really happening, or was he imagining them? "Why are they all looking at me with such aversion?" he asked himself. "Perhaps I actually am guilty, but of what? *No!* I didn't do it. I didn't. This is some scheme to drive me crazy; later they will all come out and say it was a joke. No, they really think I *am* guilty." Gawain looked at them one by one and let them see how they'd wounded him.

"Before I pass sentence," said King Basil, "do you have anything more to say for yourself?"

Gawain didn't feel like speaking. "What's the use?" he wondered. "They've made up their minds. Why waste words?"

"Well?" said the King.

Gawain hesitated some long seconds. Then he looked proudly into Basil's eyes and turned and looked at all the others and said in a ringing voice, "I am an honorable goose. How you could judge me otherwise, I do not know. Perhaps our Maker knows. Certainly He knows how much I once loved you. But now I HATE each and every living one of you, and with all my heart, for seeing evil in me that is not there. Shame on the lot of you!"

"Is that all?" asked the King.

"That is all," said Gawain.

"I hereby sentence you to imprisonment in the castle dungeon until you have the goodness to tell us where you have hidden the treasure you stole," said the King. Then to the guards: "Put him in irons!"

Gawain stared at the ground and saw his own yellow feet. They, at least, seemed real. He could feel no compassion from anyone around him. He felt leaden, benumbed. Vaguely he heard the bell in the tower strike three times. When the guards approached him carrying chains, a sudden

rage fired his spirit. He saw the wide blue sky outside the courtroom. "I will be rid of you all *forever!*" he honked loudly. He beat his wings and with a furious short run he was off the floor and flying out of a big open window.

The crowd ran out after him. They watched him soar high over the town, high above the tallest steeples and across Lake Superb. They saw him disappear into the forest on the other side. The King stood there and vowed to all gathered around him that he would track Gawain down and see that he got what was coming to him.

The real thief, the one who *should* have been on trial, had been sitting in the courtroom watching the proceedings with much emotion. He was not easily noticed because he was small. Who was he, this thief? A mouse, Derek. He was a friend of Gawain's, though he seldom saw him, tending to associate more often with creatures his own size. Several times during the trial he had wanted to come forth and announce that *he* was the thief, not Gawain, but he was afraid. At one point he felt that he was about to stand up and remind them all that the evidence against Gawain was merely circumstantial. But he couldn't do even that, because it might lead to the confession he wished he had the courage to make.

How did Derek come to be a thief? Well, the treasure house was not so entrance-proof as the King, the architect, the builders, Gawain, the other guards, and everyone else thought. True, the walls were stone a foot thick, and the floor was stone, and the only way in or out was through the heavy, well-locked, well-guarded door. The only way? Not really. Between two stones in a corner of the floor, there was one small, uncemented chink big enough for a small mouse to get through, taking something with him—and Derek discovered it.

One day, exploring an old mole run that started at his own door, he arrived right under the chink between those two stones, and like any mouse confronted with a small opening, he just had to know what was on the other side of it. Coming through, he found himself inside the Royal Treasury. He gasped at what he beheld. King Basil, who'd been there earlier, had forgotten to turn down the lamps,

and from all sides the immense treasure of his kingdom
glowed and glinted. For a long time Derek just gazed about,
overawed with the glittering abundance. He tiptoed here
and there and shyly touched a few rubies, delighting in the
red richness of their honeyed gleam. Remembering his own
digs, his home among the writhing roots of an old oak—the
sometimes damp, sometimes crumbly walls, the rickety
furniture, the bed he had recently made of a moldy piece of
burlap, the smell of stale cheese and prehistoric earth—he
was slowly overcome with sickening envy.

And a strange, perhaps not so strange, thing happened.
Though he had never in his five and a half long years of life

done anything criminal, he decided he had to have a bright red ruby, and he took one down through the chink and back to his home among the oak roots.

For several days he spent much of the time looking at his little apple, the stolen ruby, placing it now here, now there, in his home. He knew he had done something wrong, but he reasoned that a mighty king would never miss a little ruby, and though he felt bad, on the whole he felt rather more good than bad with the ruby in his possession. He soon went back to the treasury and, one at a time, he took a few more rubies. He set these where he felt they showed up to good advantage.

The place was beginning to look a lot better, and he felt somehow more like a mouse of consequence. When he went out briefly into the world, he noted that his friends treated him with more respect, perhaps because he was behaving in a more respect-commanding way.

No longer satisfied with the less than modest existence of an unimportant mouse, he went back for still more rubies, and then for more. He now owned, or at least he had in his house, twenty-nine claret-colored gems that glowed and sparkled warmly by the light of his lamps. He arranged them in various ways. First he tried them as a border around his room, but found they had to be spaced at too great intervals; it was not the effect he wanted. Next he placed them around his bed. The contrast with the burlap was startling. It had an almost humorous aspect that he liked. He wished he could share this with his cousin Jeffrey, but Jeffrey was a blabber-mouth. Too bad. He would have to enjoy it by himself.

He next discovered that lying down on his bed he couldn't see the rubies, and he wanted to be able to enjoy them from the luxury of a reclining position. He got up and scurried about, rearranging them in concentric circles in the middle of his floor. The bright red rubies made a brilliant sort of rug on the dun-colored earth. Later he sat cross-legged on his burlap bed, playing on his tiny zither, enjoying the new décor.

The treasure wasn't his, he knew it wasn't his, but

there it was on *his* floor, and it made him feel wealthy. He got up, fashioned himself a cane from a fine oak twig, and went out walking. Everyone he met said he looked very sporting carrying a cane.

That night he dreamed he was the emperor of a realm populated by small creatures like himself—mice, moles, frogs, bats, hummingbirds, and such—with large insects acting as servants. In the morning he went back to the treasury. Now he began taking bright golden ducats. He felt he was taking, not stealing, because it never occurred to him that he had become a criminal. As far as he was concerned, a criminal was a ruffian, a dangerous creature ready to harm others, someone who belonged in prison. And Derek, though he knew he was wrong, knew he was not a ruffian, and dangerous, but only Derek, a mild-mannered, goodhearted mouse.

He was a very busy rodent, plying back and forth through the old mole run carrying the heavy ducats. He was a worker, a collector, a decorator, and, when he rested, a nabob. He decided the ducats would look best on his walls. He built scaffolding and with mighty efforts he raised the ducats and pounded them into the sides of his room, using a sledgehammer covered with cloth to keep from nicking the

surface of the coins. He had to do this all by himself, lifting the ducats and holding them in place while he hammered.

The effect was glorious. In the mellow, golden glow all about him, the rubies were here and there mirrored in the ducats, and their own rubescent light was here and there gilded by reflected images of the ducats on the walls. Derek decided to light candles. This was even better than lamplight because the flickering made the ruby and gold reflections dance ecstatically, as Derek's heart beat with excitement. How utterly beautiful! If he could only share it with someone.

He picked up his cane, climbed the stairs to the outside, and scampered into town. There he walked up and down the streets pretending to be interested in the contents of shop windows, loitered on corners, saying hello to whoever passed by and knowing that he could not tell anybody what he wanted so much to tell. It had to be a secret.

If it had to be a secret, he might as well get the most out of having one. He sauntered along the boulevard with his cane under his arm and his paws in his pockets, knowing he knew something no one else did. He stopped to talk with a rabbit of his acquaintance, and as they wondered whether it was going to rain or whether the clouds were just threatening and not intending to deliver, he pictured his bejeweled home and smiled inwardly at the rabbit's ignorance.

Derek ate truffles that night. They were hard to find, but he had taken the trouble to find and dig them up. He had them with a mellow Burgundy three years old. He looked about him, satisfied. A bit of wine wet his whiskers. He wiped it. No, he was not completely satisfied. All the color in his little mansion was on the warm side—red rubies, gold ducats, brown earth, tan burlap, wood—all yellowed by candlelight. He needed some offsetting coolness in the color scheme.

He thought about this all night and in the early morning he returned to the treasure house. He was still mightily impressed with what he saw there, but no longer was he overawed. He himself now lived in a similar luxurious setting. Rummaging about, he found some silver pieces of excellent craftsmanship, including a medallion of gracefully carved lilies that he had once seen pinned to King Basil's purple robe. He took this down the hole and back to his home, and then he returned for a few more silver ornaments —a couple of rings, a brooch, and an engraved spoon as big as himself.

The silver spoon he leaned casually and artfully against

the wall by his dresser. The silver medallion he placed on top of the dresser, to serve as a sort of salver. The brooch he fastened over his door, and he hung the rings on the backs of his two chairs. Then he studied the results of his work from various viewpoints and saw that he had done well. But still, something was missing—a center of interest. He hurried back to the treasure house.

There, lifting a velvet covering, he discovered the Kalikak diamond. Its grandeur stunned him. Now that he had seen it, his own home seemed poorer again by contrast. He had to have it, no two ways about it. Tremulous with excitement, breathless, alarmed at his own audacity, yet proud of it, he began moving the large diamond. He pushed it off the table where he had found it. He rolled it along the stone floor, and when it reached the crevice, it dropped through. He rolled it along the mole run and got it into his house.

He didn't know that it was called the Kalikak diamond and that it was world-famous. He only knew how unspeakably impressive it was, flashing, radiating, almost alive. He knew where to put this awesome gem—where it belonged: on top of his rickety table in the center of the room. He managed to get it up there, and then he lighted all his lamps and candles. The Kalikak diamond not only reflected the yellow light but shot heavenly blue arrows everywhere, and the lights, the reflections, and the inter-reflections created a marvelous atmosphere that completely turned Derek's small head. His place was a palace and he was mighty proud of it. True, it still smelled of stale cheese and of everlasting earth, and it still had rags in it and rickety furniture, but it was a palace all the same.

Stuffed with cheese, wine, and mushrooms, he lay on his bed of jute that night, tossing, turning, belching, and thinking. Was it an accident that had led him through the mole run and into the treasure house, or was it Fate or some other great power? Was he not destined, being Derek, uniquely himself and no other, to come by this great good fortune? He wondered.

He fell asleep late and when he woke up he felt he had to find a confidant. There must be someone, someone he had not yet thought of, with whom he could share his secret. There must be someone he could discuss his feelings with and show off to. Of course it would have to be someone small who could fit into his home and see what he was talking about.

At noon he hastened into town; and there he learned about Gawain's trial. They were all talking about it. Everywhere.

He hurried home and flung himself on his bed. It had never really occurred to him that the robberies would be discovered. He had not let himself think about that. Sometimes he had begun to think about it, but he had quickly pushed the thought aside, and his fears with it. As long as he kept the secret, he had felt, it would remain a secret. He realized now how unrealistic that had been.

He began anxiously to consider Gawain's plight, and his considerations led to the conclusion that the good goose was safe. No one would ever believe that anyone like Gawain

had committed a crime. He had everyone's highest esteem, especially the King's. Would anyone have believed that he, Derek, had done it? Would he himself have believed it before it happened? But what if Gawain were found guilty? Well, if Gawain *were* found guilty, he, Derek the mouse, would come forward in court and point to himself as the culprit so that justice should prevail. If Gawain were found innocent, which would surely be the case, Derek decided he would keep his mouth shut.

He looked about him at his own handiwork. The golden walls seemed somewhat tarnished. The rubies had lost some of their luster. He turned and lay with his face in the burlap. He got some comfort from his own warm breath, and from the familiar, musty smell of his bed.

In the three days before the trial, Derek came to realize that he was a thief. And not just a little thief but a thief on a grand scale. And he had stolen from royalty. Why had he not understood this before? He had not allowed himself to understand it. A trial was being held because a crime had been committed, and *he* had committed the crime.

He looked in his mirror many times. He didn't look like a criminal. He looked as he always had, only sadder, more worried. Did Gawain the goose look like a criminal? Cer-

tainly not! Yet he was being brought to trial; it was considered possible that he was guilty. Derek decided he would confess. He would go straight to the King, make restitution, and take his punishment. Punishment? What punishment? Hanging in the public square? Whipping? Years in a verminous prison on a diet of stale bread and water? Banishment from the kingdom? The loss of the King's affection?

No, he would not confess. He would confess only if absolutely necessary. Only if Gawain were found guilty. And that wouldn't happen. These and similar ruminations oppressed Derek's sleepless nights and weary days until the day of the trial.

At the trial he could hardly believe what was happen-

ing. He sat in the corner of a bench alongside the rump of
Uriah the pig, clasping his hands together, biting his nails,
staring. How could the wise King make such errors of judg-
ment? How could the whole community, Gawain's friends,
turn against him? Even if he *were* guilty, were they not still
his friends? What kind of friendship were they showing?
Why didn't Gawain speak up more, defend himself? Why
did he only assert his innocence, instead of arguing his case?

Derek was convinced that if Gawain hadn't flown out
the window, he would finally have come forward and ended
the joke, the stupid injustice, by confessing. He had to
think that.

He shambled home on weak legs and sat down at his
rickety table with his head against the Kalikak diamond.
Though thoroughly depressed, he was not unmindful of the
sensation of the hard, smooth, cool diamond against his soft,
furry brow. He wished he could go back in time to the turning point, the moment inside the treasury when he was smit-
ten with envy of the King's wealth. If history could be un-
wound and he were there again, he would consider the
consequences and he wouldn't steal. Instead, he would go
straight to the King, report the existence of the crevice between the two stones in the floor so that it could be cemented,

and he would be rewarded in some way, even gain a pleasant prominence in the community.

Why had he wanted to be rich, or to feel rich? Was he an unhappy mouse before? Didn't he see the King himself often looking sad? Was anyone completely happy?

Well, Gawain had escaped; he was not being punished. Derek had at least that to be thankful for. He decided to cheer himself up with some music. He got his zither and sat down to play. A few times he strummed lightly on the strings. His plectrum fell from his fingers. He was overpowered by misery.

Weeks passed. Derek sat in his hole among the oak roots, not eating, not doing anything, staring at the foolish ducats sticking in his walls. Sometimes he lay like a corpse on his burlap bed, and whenever he was unable to abide his own company a second longer, he went into town. His friends said he looked unwell and ought to see a good doctor. He kept hearing that the King's scouts were searching for Gawain all over the forest on the other side of Lake Superb, where he had disappeared.

At home he began wondering about Gawain again. Wherever he was, was he happy? Derek hadn't faced this question. Now it was plain that he couldn't possibly be

happy. Would any innocent creature be who had been con-
demned by society and forced to flee like a criminal? Of
course not! He was somewhere all by himself, hurt and in
hiding. Derek thought of a scheme to clear the goose's
name. He would go on stealing. Then they would realize
that they had been mistaken about Gawain.

In the next few days he went back to the treasury
and stole at random—gems, medals, money, whatever—
and piled the things up in his home. In town he soon learned
that the new thefts had been discovered and that there was
no one to blame now because only King Basil had keys. It
was a mystery. But at last everyone knew for certain that
Gawain was innocent and had suffered a grave injustice.
They all went about with their heads hanging in shame.
The King was devastated. All he could do was scowl at
his Prime Minister, offer a large reward for whoever
discovered the real thief, and double the forces combing
the woods for Gawain.

Vindicating Gawain was the first good work Derek had
done since he'd become a thief. It eased his misery, but only
briefly. All he had to do was think of the unhappiness he had
caused in the royal household and in all the King's subjects,
and realize that the restoring of Gawain's reputation was

still no help to Gawain himself, and he fell into paralyzing despair.

He had to do something, to accomplish something, to assuage his feelings of guilt. It struck him that he needn't have done more stealing to establish Gawain's innocence. He could just as well have put the stuff back. Little by little he began carting the loot from his home to the treasury. It was hard labor, but knowing it was the right thing to do gave him strength.

He began to eat again so he could work better, and working, in turn, made him hungry. In one day he took down the gold ducats and hauled them back to the treasure house. The next day he brought back all the rubies and the Kalikak diamond. The third day he returned the rest.

The news spread quickly through the town. Wherever Derek went, it was being discussed with great wonder and puzzlement, in the tavern, on the streets, everywhere. Derek pretended great interest when the subject was broached to him. He also learned that the King's scouts had given up searching for Gawain in the forest. They had decided he was not there and they were starting to look farther afield. Perhaps their efforts were useless. Perhaps he had flown to a distant land.

The return of the treasure did not restore anyone's happiness. After the initial excitement, it hardly seemed to matter. What mattered was what had been done to Gawain, and everyone knew that it had to be righted or no one would ever feel glad to be himself again. Little thought went to finding the thief.

The "thief" sat in his poor den, staring at the indentations the gold ducats had left on his earthen walls. If he were happy now, he could feel at home again in this modest hole. But he was far from happy. Since all the treasure had been returned, perhaps he was no longer a thief. And Gawain's name had been cleared—but he knew that Gawain was miserable. He knew that King Basil was miserable, that everyone in his realm was miserable, and that he, Derek, was the sole cause of it. Tears blurred his eyes. The pall of gloom that hung over the whole kingdom hung thickest over him.

When Gawain escaped through the courthouse window and flew high above the town on great, wild wingstrokes, he looked back below. From the height of the free sky, the King and the crowd gathered around him in the courthouse square looked like frenzied insects. Gawain resolved to get away from them as far as he possibly could.

Flying over Lake Superb, he welcomed the coolness of the open air and the vista of the wide, forest-bordered waters. But he was a tired goose after his recent ordeals, and he soon used up the energy provided by his anger.

When he had crossed the lake, he could go no farther, and he dropped into an open space in the woods. He rested against a hickory tree, breathing heavily and sensing his new surroundings. He had been in many places before, in this forest and in others, but as he had not been in this particular spot, it looked strange. It also looked familiar, because it was just a place in a forest.

He had not eaten the poor fare offered him in prison, and he was hungry, yet too tired to forage for food. He found a bed of rhododendron, burrowed under the leaves, and, fairly well concealed, he fell asleep.

When he woke in the morning, he was surprised to see the rhododendron leaves above him. He quickly got his bearings, preened his feathers from force of habit, and went to look for breakfast. He moved warily by the edge of the lake, since he knew he would be hunted. He found some worms to eat, some tender shoots of forest plants, and some succulent bugs.

Realizing that he must be careful not to leave tracks, he

tied rushes to his webbed feet and walked about obliterating the imprints he had made in the damp soil at the margin of the lake.

As he wandered clumsily in his strange shoes, he thought about the past few days, especially about the day of the trial, and he was sick at heart. He felt he should take off again, continue on his way to some far place, but he was too depressed for such an undertaking.

In the woods he came to a cliff, and he found in the side of it a small entrance to a rather large cave. There was light in the cave because high above the entrance was a fissure in the jagged rocks that formed a very narrow window. Gawain decided to make this cave his home for the time being, until he was sure exactly what to do, where to go.

This decision made, he got busy. With a stick and a flat stone for tools, he dug up some bushes and cleverly planted them in front of the entrance to his new home so that it would be almost impossible to see. He covered the newly dug earth with dead leaves. No one was likely to notice the narrow window, because of its position and because, from below, it looked like just another crack in the rocks.

By lashing logs and sticks together with pliable vines, he managed to make a crude chair and table. He had a home; and he felt sure that the search parties of the King, who were already looking for him in the forest, would not find it.

Gawain took up the life of a fugitive and a recluse, with only himself for company. Much as swimming gave him comfort, he would wait for night, when there was little chance of his being seen, to swim in the lake. He wore the rushes on his feet when he walked, and searched quickly and furtively for food, always hurrying back with it to his hidden cave. He avoided making a fire, though he often wanted the warmth of one and knew how to rub two sticks together until they ignited.

Mostly he stayed in the cave. And he spent his time

there brooding—savoring his miseries. He recalled his one-
time friends, remembered their looks, their voices, their
ways, the warm feeling that had existed among them. How
ever could they have turned on him, believed him a criminal
—even if the evidence did seem to prove it? How he had admired the King! Hadn't he agreed to guard the King's treasure only out of love? Weren't there millions of things he
would have preferred to do? Where was the King's gratitude? Gratitude? Love? Loyalty? Friendship? What did
such things mean to them?

Sifting his bitter recollections, he often wept with his head on his wing at his rude, homemade table, or stared at the damp stone walls. Sometimes in the middle of the night, in the darkness of his secret cave, he woke up in tears. No, now he knew: if they had ever sincerely loved him, they would have realized it was impossible for him to steal, lie, or cheat in any way. When he was extremely young, a gosling, he had lied in a small inconsequential matter, only out of fear, and maybe once, or twice, he had stolen a plum or a penny. But he was no liar, no thief.

How he yearned for friendship. How he longed to be in a community with other loving souls again. *You are a disgrace to this kingdom!* He couldn't forget that cruel sentence spoken by the King. It stuck in his brain. Why did the world go on being so beautiful in spite of the ugliness he

had experienced? The lake was beautiful, serenely beautiful. The forest was beautiful, greenly beautiful. Lake and forest, the whole shimmering world was painfully beautiful. He loved this world, but he was too hurt to enjoy it.

The King's scouts passed his hidden doorway many times. Peeping out from the cave, Gawain watched them as they beat about in the underbrush and moved on. He recognized every one of them, and sometimes he wanted to rush out and give himself up just to be able to talk again. After several weeks, they no longer appeared. They were looking elsewhere, and with a new purpose. They wanted to find him only to make amends. But Gawain didn't know that.

He was beginning to get accustomed to his new environment. He made some improvements in his dwelling—he added a footstool and a carpet he wove out of rushes. He still bitterly remembered the injustices he had endured, but he bravely went on living, and even managed to enjoy it ever so slightly. Had he been able to share his unhappiness with a friend, he would have been happier.

With no one searching for him now, he was more lonesome, but a bit more relaxed. He still wore the rushes tied to his feet and he still kept a wary eye, but he stayed longer out of his cave and wandered farther in the daylight, studying things, such as the great variety of berries, thinking less about himself. He felt fairly safe.

One day, extending his researches into a new corner of his domain, he was suddenly confronted with the mouse Derek, who emerged from under a large leaf. Gawain was electrified. He had given up the idea of ever again seeing anyone from his past life.

"Gawain!" shouted Derek in his thin, shrill voice.

Gawain stood still, fastened to the ground. "Derek!" he whispered hoarsely, staring at his old friend, amazed he could still talk after his long silence. "What are *you* doing here?"

"I've been looking for you," said Derek.

Gawain laughed, or rather he made some sounds meant to be laughter. "I suppose you are going to subdue me, put me in irons, and bring me back to justice," he said sarcastically.

"Oh, no," said Derek. "The only reason they're still searching for you is that they want to ask your forgiveness. The King, everyone—they know it wasn't you."

After a measure of silence, Gawain asked, "Do they know who it was?"

"No," said Derek. "They don't know. But I do. It was *me!*"

"*You!*"

"Yes, me," said Derek.

"How do they know it wasn't I?" asked Gawain, staring at the little mouse in astonishment.

"Because," said Derek, "I went on stealing after you flew away—to establish your innocence." And he told Gawain the whole story, of his thieving without malicious intent, his shock at Gawain's being found guilty at the trial, his wanting to confess and being afraid to, his suffering.

Sometimes he stopped to cry, and when he found that he was able to cry more in the presence of the one he had wronged than he'd been able to by himself, his little body was racked with sobs. Gawain broke down and cried with him, the hot tears coursing down his neck. He felt so many emotions—joy at having been vindicated and at being with Derek, anger at what had happened, misery that such things *could* happen, pity for Derek, bitterness toward his faithless friends and toward the King he had loved, longing for a good life, sweetness at thinking how beautiful it could be, and sorrow that it wasn't so. It was all too much for him.

"Can you ever forgive me?" asked Derek, forlorn.

Gawain looked at the small mouse cowering by his rush-shod feet. "I forgive you gladly, dear mouse," he said. "I can see how much you've suffered, and we both know what suffering is. But never will I forgive those who used to call themselves my friends—these trees are more my friends than they were—and I'm certain I will never pardon the King."

"But they've suffered too," said Derek, "and the King most of all."

"Let him suffer. Let them all suffer," said Gawain. "I never want to see any of them again." But he did want to see them again, there was nothing he wanted more, and the mouse knew it. He lightly touched Gawain's grooved leg. That did it. Feeling the touch of a fellow creature, the warmth he'd been starved for so long, he relented. "Yes, I do want to see them," he admitted. "I want it very much. I forgive them."

"We all make mistakes," said Derek.

"Come and see my home," said Gawain. On the way he explained his funny, rush footwear. Derek laughed and Gawain undid the rushes. They had a pleasant meal in the cave

and talked of many things. "Why did you look for me here," Gawain asked, "when all the others had given up looking in these woods?"

"A hunch," said Derek. "I thought you must be terribly dejected, and I knew that in your place I would not have had the heart to fly very far just yet. I guessed you were here somewhere in hiding, and I felt I was meant to find you. I rowed across this morning—you weren't long in turning up."

Gawain laughed. "Of all those who've looked for me, you were the one I was least likely to notice, especially hidden under a leaf. Tell me, are you going to confess?"

"Yes," said Derek, "the treasure has been returned, and when I come back with you, they will be so happy they won't want to punish me too severely. But I must be punished for what I did. Right?"

"I think you *have* been punished for what you did," said Gawain. "You've suffered more than anyone."

"No, *you* did," said Derek. "You were the one wrongfully blamed."

"But you had it on your conscience that you caused the suffering of so many," said Gawain.

"What about the King?" said Derek. "Think what *he's* been through after judging you so unjustly!"

Gawain sighed.

"Derek," he said, "they must never know who did it.

Let them always wonder and never know the answer. They deserve at least that for their lack of faith."

"I agree," said Derek readily. "Only you and I will know."

They started across the lake about midday, Derek riding on Gawain's back. He held on tightly because there was a wind and the water was choppy. They arrived in town at sunset when the lights were being turned on. It was as if the lights were going on to welcome them.

When they suddenly appeared, walking up the main avenue to the King's palace, like a triumphant army coming to claim its trophies, everyone ran to see them and shouted and cheered and went racing around proclaiming the news to everyone else.

They were joyfully received by the King. "I will never, from now to eternity, mistrust you again! I repent," he said to Gawain, and he meant it.

"Please forget it, I beg you, your highness," said Gawain. "I forgive." Relieved of his heavy sorrow, the King began crying. He had never cried in public before, but he was unashamed. He embraced Gawain in a mighty, loving hug;

he embraced Derek with a bit more care. They responded in kind. After a long session together in which they discussed the robbery, the trial, its aftermath, and everyone's feelings, not to mention the various problems of living—as a bear, a goose, a mouse, a king, a subject—Gawain returned to his real home and Derek to his. The whole town slept well that night.

A party was held to celebrate Gawain's homecoming and to honor him, and also Derek, who had succeeded in finding him. One by one, Gawain's friends took him aside to ask his forgiveness, and he freely forgave them. He was able to love them again, but he loved them now in a wiser way, knowing their weakness. The King told Derek he intended to give him a reward, but Derek begged him not to.

The treasury was now being guarded by four bulldogs, the son of Louisa May who had been named after Gawain, and his three brothers, Gabriel, Giles, and Ichabod. The King appointed Gawain to the office of Royal Architect. Gawain made Derek his assistant, and got to work at once on his first project—a new opera house, for which he decided to use his favorite form, the egg. He wanted to make buildings that would be celebrated as great architecture long after his own lifetime.

Before starting to work for Gawain, Derek secretly cemented the chink in the floor of the treasury. It wasn't really necessary, but it made him feel better. He felt it put an end to the whole episode—the theft, the trial, its aftermath.

There was peace and harmony in the kingdom once again, except for the little troubles that come up every so often even in the best of circumstances, since nothing is perfect.